The True Story of Critter Angels

By Yani

These wise and noble creatures
— friends, companions, teachers —
keep watch as they patiently mentor
us so we may grow in love, respect,
understanding and compassion
toward all beings.

The True Story of Critter Angels
Story and Illustrations by Yani (and Shendl Diamond)
Copyright © 2005 Shendl Diamond. All rights reserved.

Quantity discounts are available on bulk purchases of this book. For information please contact LikeMinds Press, Inc. at www.likemindspress.com.

Library of Congress Control Number: 2005905162
ISBN 0-9764724-3-0 (ISBN-13 978-0-9764724-3-8)
Printed in Hong Kong
First Edition: October 2005

Dedicated to Vashti, Punkin, Nellie, Zahava, Champie, Robert the Cat, Little One, Annie, Max, Nelson, Delta, Moi, Jessica, June, Omie, Tig, Lindy, Pickle, Torrey, Kapper, Cookie, Josie, Wanda and all the other critter angels.

The True Story
of Critter Angels

By Yani

My name is Yani. I'm an angel, a kitty angel.

I live and work here on earth and

my sole reason for being here is to love you.

Let me try to explain.

You see, there are dog angels and horse angels, bird angels and bunny angels, turtle angels and guinea pig angels, and, well, you probably get the idea.

There are critter angels of every shape and size.

Our angel wings don't usually show
when we're living here with you on earth.

It's supposed to be a secret.

Our wings are always there,

you just can't see them.

Sometimes children can see our wings,
but only when they are very young.
Then someone teaches them
that they can't see our wings,
so they forget that they really can.

We're here to love you
and to help you open your hearts to love.

Our love is unconditional
and our hope is to share our love with you
so that your hearts will open and your love
will grow toward all beings,
especially each other.

Once you love someone, your hearts form a special and invisible bond that never goes away. Your love builds a connection, a link, that lives on forever inside your heart. This is true for critters and for people, too.

And while we're here to love you and
help open your hearts to love,
we also need you.

We need you to care for us
and love us
and feed us
and watch out for us.

Part of the reason I'm sharing this with you is so you'll understand why we're here and why sometimes we have to leave.

Before I continue, there are some

other critter angels

who would like to meet you.

This is Rudy. She works with me.

We are in charge of loving

the same family.

She wanted me to show you

her picture so you could

see that there really are

other critter angels out there.

This is Easy. He's my brother and yes, that's really his name. When he was a baby he was very sick, but he was such an easy patient to care for his name soon became Easy.

Easy loves being a critter angel. His specialty is teaching love and compassion. I was lucky to get this picture of him with his wings showing.

Sara is a dog angel. She loves showing off her wings so she allowed me to take her picture. She thought you should see other critter angels, not just the cats. Sara is an expert at enthusiastically sharing her unconditional love for others.

This is Torrey. She wanted you to know that she was blessed to live with an amazing family that loved her deeply and she loved them with all her heart. When she had to leave they were very sad and so was she. She hated leaving them. It didn't seem fair.

She wants her family to know that she's safe — that she's watching over them, loving them and protecting them each and every moment.

You see, even though it makes us very sad to leave you

because you mean so much to us, sometimes we're needed back in heaven.

When we're called, we must go. It usually means that some other human heart needs our special gift.

We have so many humans to love and watch over, sometimes we have to leave even our favorite and most special people sooner than expected.

Even though we know
you'll be sad when we have to leave,
we need you to know that we're OK.
We'll miss you very much but
we will always be watching over you.

The most important part is that
we will always be with you inside your heart.

All you have to do is close your eyes and think of us and you'll feel us right there with you. Your heart will fill with a warm glow and you will know that we're here.

You might feel our soft breath or even the touch of our little wet nose on your cheek.

But no matter what...

we are right here with you,
because when you love a critter angel
we will be with you forever and ever,
no matter what!

That's just the way it is

when you love a critter angel.

Thank you for loving us!

Please use the rest of these pages
for pictures of all your critter angels.

Don't worry if their wings
don't show in the pictures —
you know their wings
are there.

My critter angel photo

My critter angel photo

My critter angel photo

My critter angel photo

Dedicated to all the critter angels who have been called away and to those who still live here with us. Thank you for watching over us and for teaching us the meaning of forgiveness and unconditional love.

Thank you for inspiring this book.

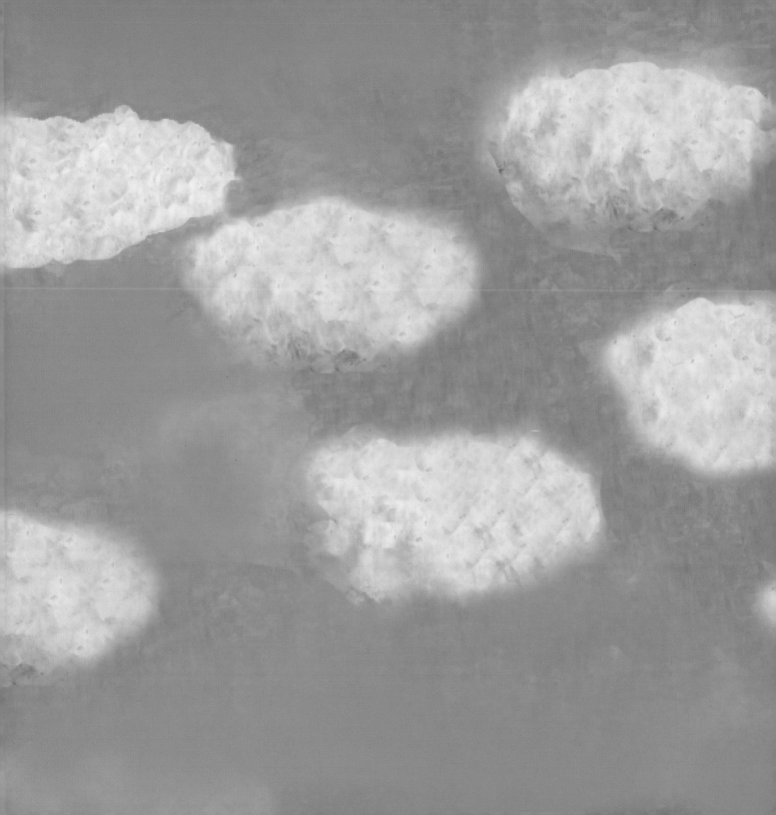